E VIS
Viscardi, Dolly, 1950-
All around cats
32050003868335

WITHDRAWN

This book belongs to:

_____

D1472315

The illustrations were created digitally on a Macintosh using Adobe Illustrator
The text and display type were set in Dom Casual and Improv
Composed in the United States of America
Designed by Lois A. Rainwater
Edited by Aimee Jackson

Text © 2004 by Dolly Viscardi
Illustrations © 2004 by David Brooks

Books for Young Readers
NorthWord Press
18705 Lake Drive East
Chanhassen, MN 55317
www.northwordpress.com

All rights reserved. No part of this work covered by the copyrights herein may be reproduced or used in any form or by any means—graphic, electronic or mechanical, including photocopying, recording, and taping of information on storage and retrieval systems—without the prior written permission of the publisher.

Library of Congress Cataloging-in-Publication Data

Viscardi, Dolly, date.
All around cats / by Dolly Viscardi ; illustrated by David Brooks.
p. cm.
Summary: Rhyming text describes a variety of cats and their activities.
ISBN 1-55971-072-1 (hc with dust jacket)
[1. Cats--Fiction. 2. Stories in rhyme.] I. Brooks, David, date- ill. II. Title.

PZ8.3.V733Al 2004

[E]--dc22
2004002889

Printed in Singapore
10 9 8 7 6 5 4 3 2 1

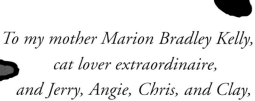
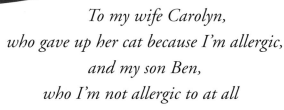

To my mother Marion Bradley Kelly,
cat lover extraordinaire,
and Jerry, Angie, Chris, and Clay,
who have learned
a little appreciation for cats

—D.V.

To my wife Carolyn,
who gave up her cat because I'm allergic,
and my son Ben,
who I'm not allergic to at all

—D.B.

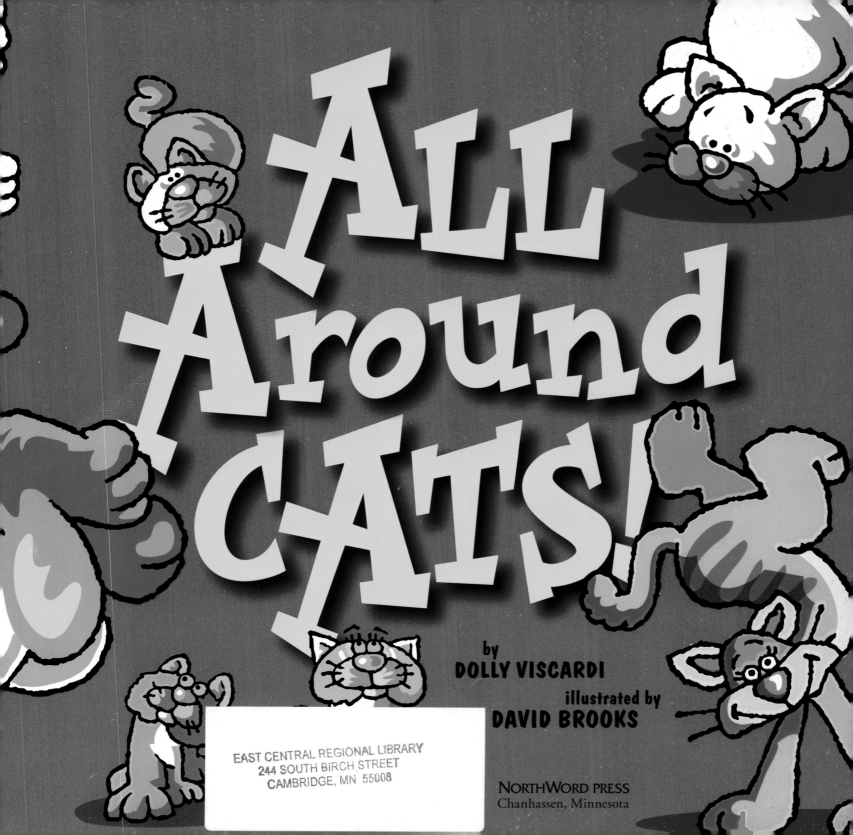

ALL Around CATS!

by
DOLLY VISCARDI

illustrated by
DAVID BROOKS

EAST CENTRAL REGIONAL LIBRARY
244 SOUTH BIRCH STREET
CAMBRIDGE, MN 55008

NORTHWORD PRESS
Chanhassen, Minnesota

Inside, outside, upside, downside,
round about, in and out, **ALL AROUND CATS!**

Striped tabby, no-tail,

calico female,

tree jumpers,

Swing gliders, ledge hiders, alley prowlers, roof howlers, can crashers, bubble bashers, ALL AROUND CATS!

Tail switchers,

nose twitchers,

eye blinkers,

leg slinkers,

floor pouncers,

bed bouncers,
ALL
AROUND
CATS!

BAIT

Window peepers,

corner creepers,

screen sliders,
low riders,

silent sneakers, door peekers,
ALL AROUND CATS!

night trappers,

people pleasers,

puppy teasers,
ALL
AROUND
CATS!

Milk drinkers, quick thinkers,
table hoppers, crumb droppers,
whisker wipers, face swipers, **ALL AROUND CATS!**

Morning posers,

evening dozers,

pillow testers,

basket nesters,

noisy singers, bell ringers,

ALL AROUND
CATS!

DOLLY VISCARDI is a first-time author who teaches preschool. She has been an elementary-school reading and literacy specialist for many years, and loves to read and write. When she is not teaching or writing, she hikes and skis in the mountains near Meeker, Colorado, where she lives with her family. Although she grew up in a house filled with felines, these days she is in-between cats.

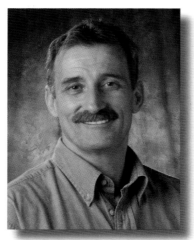

DAVID BROOKS lives in Long Beach, California, with his wife, Carolyn, and son, Benjamin. He is a graduate of the University of Maine and has worked as an illustrator, designer, art director, and creative director. David started illustrating full-time in 1997. You can see more of his work at www.theispot.com/artist/djbrooks.